Lighthouse Victory

Columbus, OH

SRAonline.com

An Open Court Curriculum.

Printed in China.

Send all inquiries to this address:
SRA/McGraw-Hill
4400 Easton Commons
Columbus, OH 43219

ISBN: 978-0-07-608754-9
MHID: 0-07-608754-9

1 2 3 4 5 6 7 8 9 NOR 13 12 11 10 09 08 07

The McGraw·Hill Companies

My name is Rebecca Bates, and I live in Scituate, Massachusetts, a harbor town located near Boston. Its early settlers, in 1628, were shipbuilders and fishers. Most of the townspeople still are. My father, Captain Simeon Bates, is neither.

My father is the lighthouse keeper. The lighthouse helps lost sailors find their way home. During storms or when the guiding stars are covered by clouds, its light leads boats safely to shore.

But since the war began in 1812, two years ago, the lighthouse is important for another reason. It also serves as a watchtower to spot any enemy British ships that might enter the harbor.

For two years the British have sailed here from England to attack American ships. When the British soldiers need supplies and food, they come ashore in small boats. These invaders go into harbor towns like Scituate and begin looting. They think they can take whatever they want.

Last week my father decided it was time to head into town to gather food and supplies for the long winter ahead. Most of our seven brothers and sisters went with him, but Father said Mother, my sister Abigail, and I could stay. He told us girls we were in charge of the lighthouse while he was away!

After they had gone, Abigail and I climbed the ladder high into the lighthouse. We watched, aloft, as our family made its way into town. From way up there, we could see our sleepy town several miles away.

Since we were in charge, Abigail and I decided to wash the lighthouse windows. We had helped Father do it many times before. Sometimes he let us light the lantern too.

As we worked I looked out across the water. It was such a lovely autumn day! The idea that British soldiers could be on their way to our quiet harbor never crossed my thoughts.

Of course Father had told us what to do if we see invaders' boats. We were to alert the captain of the militia.

Scituate's militia often drills in the woods near the lighthouse. They march out from town to the woods to practice. The music always lets us know when the militia is marching. Young boys who march along play a fife, or flute, and beat a drum.

Abigail and I knew that we were supposed to alert the captain, but we were still startled when we saw a ship in the harbor later that day.

As the late afternoon had turned to dusk, it had become harder to see. Abigail and I strained our eyes to search the harbor. Suddenly we both saw them: small boats were coming toward shore carrying soldiers. The buttons on their uniforms glinted in the remaining light.

We had no time to warn the militia. The boats were coming much too quickly, and the town was too far away. The invaders would have been ashore before we could have gotten to town, and there would not be enough time for the militia captain to gather his men. By then the invaders would be ashore, hiding in the woods.

I watched in dismay as the small boats drew closer to land. If we could not warn the town, we had to find some way to stop the invaders. But what could the two of us do against trained soldiers?

Then Abigail cried, "Rebecca, how I wish I could hear the sound of our militia's fife and drum coming from town right now!"

Suddenly I had a plan for stopping the soldiers. I gave Abigail a quick hug, hurried down the lighthouse ladder, and ran to our living quarters.

Abigail thundered down the ladder behind me.

I grabbed our fife and drum. We had not wanted to learn to play them, but now I was so happy that Mother had made us learn! After telling Mother to stay in the lighthouse for safety, I grabbed Abigail's hand and took her to hide among the cedar trees.

Once in the trees, I gave the drum to Abigail. She asked, "What are we doing? We should be inside where it's safe."

I did not answer her. It was almost dark. The soldiers' boats were coming closer by the moment. It was time to put my plan into action.

As we huddled in the trees, I told Abigail to beat the drum in the same rhythm that our militia's drummer did.

"What? Why?" Abigail asked with a look of terror on her face.

"Just do it, Abigail! There is no time to explain!" I said.

She began to beat out the steady rhythm on the drum. I picked up the fife and played "Yankee Doodle." I had heard the militia's fife player play the song many times. I was so nervous that I missed several notes at first. As the song went on, though, my playing grew stronger and louder.

The branches of the cedar trees swayed gently in the chilly breeze. I shivered, but was it because I was cold or afraid? I was not certain.

I thought, *It must work. It simply must!* I desperately hoped that the soldiers wanted to avoid a battle. Perhaps if they thought the militia was on its way, they would return to their ship.

The sounds of military music drifted on the evening air, from the woods down to the beach and out across the water. I could barely see the soldiers leaning forward in their boats, straining to hear the tune. Beside me, Abigail steadily beat the drum while I played the song again.

The soldiers suddenly stopped rowing. The water in the harbor rocked their boats back and forth as they listened closer still.

Abigail and I played on, getting louder by the moment. She understood now what I hoped to achieve. With the growing dark and the dense trees, the soldiers could not see if the militia was coming. If the music became louder, it would seem as though the militia was drawing closer to the beach, ready for battle.

The officer in the lead boat turned to look back at their ship. It was then that he noticed the raised flag that was the signal to retreat. The officer waved his arm over his head, yelling, "Retreat!"

"Oh, thank goodness!" Abigail whispered to me. They really believed that our militia was on the way to fight them!

Still playing the fife and beating the drum, we watched as the soldiers turned their boats around and headed back toward their ship.

Abigail and I were so excited to see the soldiers retreat that we played even louder than before. Our music floated out over the water, chasing the fleeing soldiers back to sea.

We waited to stop playing until the ship began moving out of the harbor toward the sea. Then, still sitting on the ground among the trees, Abigail and I hugged each other tightly.

After the ship disappeared, we returned to our home. We lit the oil for the flame in the lighthouse. It burned brightly as a beacon both for boats and for our family's return trip from town. It was late into the night when our brothers and sisters burst through the door.

Father wasted no time in asking how things had been in his absence. Abigail told him about the invaders. Mother told him how Abigail and I had played the fife and drum. Then I told him how the music had deceived the soldiers and that they had fled.

Father gathered us in his arms and kissed both of us. He said it was quite an accomplishment that the two of us turned back the British army! He immediately sent a message to the town's militia captain, telling him that the British were nearby. He also told him that Abigail and I had chased away the British army with just a fife and a drum.

I returned the instruments to their room, and Abigail and I returned to our daily lives and chores. But we will always be remembered by the townspeople as their army of two.

Vocabulary

invaders (in vād´ ərz) (page 4) *n.* Plural form of **invader:** A person who breaks into something or some place without being asked or wanted.

looting (lo͞ot´ ing) (page 4) *v.* Stealing valuable things from others.

aloft (ə lôft´) (page 5) *adj.* Far above the ground.

militia (mə lish´ ə) (page 6) *n.* A group of citizens trained to fight and help in emergencies.

retreat (ri trēt´) (page 12) *v.* To move back.

accomplishment (ə kom´ plish ment) (page 14) *n.* Achievement.

Comprehension Focus: Cause and Effect

1. What caused the soldiers to retreat to their ship?
2. What effect did Abigail's statement about wanting to hear the militia's fife and drum have on Rebecca?